Meg Mackintosh

and

The Case of the Missing Babe Ruth Baseball

A Solve-It-Yourself Mystery

by Lucinda Landon

Secret Passage Press
North Scituate Rhode Island

Books by Lucinda Landon:

Meg Mackintosh and The Case of the Missing Babe Ruth Baseball
Meg Mackintosh and The Case of the Curious Whale Watch
Meg Mackintosh and The Mystery at the Medieval Castle
Meg Mackintosh and The Mystery at Camp Creepy
Meg Mackintosh and The Mystery in the Locked Library
Meg Mackintosh and The Mystery at the Soccer Match
Meg Mackintosh and The Mystery on Main Street
American History Mysteries

About the author

Lucinda Landon has been an avid mystery fan since her childhood.
She lives in Rhode Island with her husband, two sons, two dogs, two cats and
two horses. Their old house has a secret passage. For more clues and
information on how to order books, visit www.megmackintosh.com.

For information:
Secret Passage Press, 26 Tucker Hollow, N. Scituate, Rhode Island 02857

First Secret Passage Press Edition

The characters and events in this book are fictitious. Any similarity to real
persons, living or dead, is coincidental and not intended by the author.

Library of Congress Cataloging-in-Publication Data

Landon, Lucinda.
    Meg Mackintosh and the case of the missing Babe Ruth baseball: a solve-it-yourself
mystery / by Lucinda Landon.

    Summary: Meg follows a series of notes hidden in her grandfather's house to solve an
old mystery of a missing baseball signed by Babe Ruth. The reader is challenged to interpret
each clue before Meg solves it.
    (1. Mystery and detective stories. 2. Literary recreations) I. Title.
PZ7.L231735Me 1986 (Fic) 85-20055

ISBN 1-888695-00-5

(previously published by Little, Brown and Company ISBN 0-316-51318-0)

10 9 8 7 6 5 4 3

PRINTED IN THE UNITED STATES OF AMERICA

For James, Alexander, Eric,
and our grandparents

"Hmm, I do detect a bit of family resemblance," said Meg Mackintosh, as she examined Gramps's old family photo album.

"You've got some funny-looking relatives," remarked Liddy. "And look at these pictures of you and Peter!"

Meg turned another page.

"Gramps, who's this?"

"That's me," explained Gramps, "and that's my cousin Alice. She was always bossing me around. She used to drive me crazy, teasing me about my little dog and calling me 'Georgie Porgie.' I called her 'Tattletale Al' because she was always getting me in trouble.

"I'll never forget the day that photo was taken. We went on a picnic," Gramps reminisced. "That was the day she lost my prize possession."

"What was it?" Meg asked.

"My baseball, signed by the Babe himself."

"A baby signed your baseball?"

"Of course not. Babe Ruth, the greatest baseball player ever. He autographed the ball and gave it to my father and my father gave it to me. I took it to that picnic and Alice lost it. I never saw it again."

Meg examined the photo.

Alice *did* look like a troublemaker. Then Meg spied something else.

The corner of a piece of paper was sticking out from behind the old photograph. Meg pulled it out and carefully unfolded it.

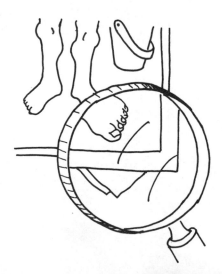

August 1928

Dear Georgie Porgie,
Summer is over, it went so fast,
Too bad your poison ivy had to last.
Sorry I scared you in the hay.
What a pity your kitty ran away.
And the time you hated me most of all,
The day I lost your precious baseball!
Well here's a mystery, here's a clue,
Maybe I can make it up to you.
The answer could be with you right now,
But you wouldn't know it anyhow.
Your cousin
Alice

Clue one
Not a father
Not a gander
Take a look
In her book

8

"Hear that, Gramps? Maybe your baseball's not lost. Just follow the clue!" exclaimed Meg.

"I doubt it's that simple, Meg-O. Just another of her pranks. I saw that note years ago, but I couldn't make head nor tail of it," Gramps sighed.

"It's probably too old to make sense now," added Liddy.

"But it might really mean something. I've got to investigate," insisted Meg.

Just then the phone rang.

"Hey, Nut-Meg, Peter here. Remind Gramps that I'll be there in the morning."

"Take your time. I've found a mystery. Something to do with a Babe Ruth baseball," Meg teased.

"A Babe Ruth baseball? That's worth a fortune! Don't touch anything until I get there!" shouted Peter.

"Tough luck, Sherlock, I can solve this one myself. Bye."

Upstairs in Gramps's boyhood room, where Meg always stayed, she took out her notebook and pencil.

"Finally. The chance I've been waiting for!" Meg told Liddy. "Peter won't let me join his Detective Club until I have 'proof' that I can solve a mystery."

"Well, you'd better do it before he gets here tomorrow," warned Liddy. "He'll never give you a chance."

Meg knew Liddy was right. She sat down at the desk and started a list.

CLUE ONE
Not a father
Not a gander
Take a look
In her book
*? Not a father?

brother	cousin
sister	baby
mother	Grandma
aunt	uncle??

Not a gander?

duck	chick
geese	hen
duckling	goose
robin	rooster

Take a look
In her book?

"Take a look in her book." Meg looked at the clue again. "Alice's diary? A nature book about birds?" She gazed up at the shelf of Gramps's old books.

10

"The Old Woman and the Little Red Hen," Liddy suggested as she squinted at the dusty titles. "Doesn't that fit?"

"I don't think so," said Meg, still jotting in her notebook. Suddenly she reached for a book. "I think I've got it!"

WHICH BOOK DID MEG REACH FOR?

"Not a father, that's mother. Not a gander, that's goose. The Mother Goose book!" Meg explained.
She carefully opened it.

Contents

Baa Baa Black Sheep
Three Blind Mice
Jack Sprat
The Cat and the Fiddle
Georgie Porgie
Little Miss Muffet
Rub a dub dub
Humpty Dumpty
The Queen of Hearts
Mary, Mary, Quite Contrary
Little Boy Blue
Wee Willie Winkie

This Book Belongs to
George Mackintosh
Christmas 1926

"This is definitely Gramps's old book. We must be on the right track," Meg said. After a moment she added, "I think I know where to look."

WHICH RHYME DID MEG TURN TO?

"Georgie Porgie, pudding and pie . . ." said Meg.

"Kissed the girls and made them cry . . ." added Liddy as she twirled a pencil in her hair. "So?"

"Georgie Porgie. That's what Alice called Gramps," Meg reminded her. Sure enough there was a small note tucked tightly between the pages. Another clue!

Clue two
Little boy blue
with the cows
in the corn
Whatever you do
Don't blow this ?

"Little boy blue, come blow your horn," Meg recited.

"But what does a horn have to do with a baseball?" wondered Liddy.

"I don't know yet. First we have to find the horn. Let's see. Foghorn? Cow horn? Horn of plenty? Cape Horn?"

"Well, good luck with it. I have to get home," Liddy said.

Meg walked Liddy downstairs, then went to find Gramps.

"Gramps, did you ever play any musical instrument, like a French horn?"

"No, but I can sing a little. Why?" Gramps replied.

"I found another clue. Alice hid it in your old Mother Goose book, on the Georgie Porgie page. It has something to do with a horn."

"That's easy." Gramps grinned as he pointed to

the bookshelf. Meg followed his finger to the old bugle there. She took it down to inspect it. She removed the mouthpiece, shook it, and peered inside with her flashlight. But no clue.

Gramps got up from the couch. "Well, my dear detective, it's time to turn in. I wouldn't get my hopes up over these clues. Old Alice, she was a sly one."

"Maybe this isn't going to be as easy as I thought," Meg whispered to Skip as they went upstairs to bed.

Meg checked her detective kit. Everything was in order — a magnifying glass, a pair of tweezers to pick up small clues, flashlight and extra batteries, tape measure, scissors, envelopes, and, of course, her detective notebook and pencils.

"I have to be sure to write everything down," she

THE YOUNG DETECTIVE'S HANDBOOK

said to Skip as she got under the covers. "The tiniest fact can solve the biggest mystery. Track, write, decode, deduce ... then I'll have plenty of proof to show Peter and his Detective Club." After a while she slid her notebook under her pillow and dozed off to sleep.

"Yikes," shrieked Meg. "Stop! Please stop that awful noise!"

Gramps put the bugle down. "If you think that's bad, Meg-O, you should have heard your father play it. I got this bugle for him when he went to Scout Camp. He was a pitiful horn player. Ah well, rise and shine for breakfast."

When Meg got downstairs, Gramps was making pancakes. "All this talk about Alice reminds me of when we were kids. Once she challenged me to a pancake-eating contest. I ate sixteen, while she watched with a miserable grin on her face. When it was her turn, she ate three and forfeited the contest. She had decided from the start to let me win. All I won was a stomachache!" Gramps laughed. "Alice was always getting the best of me."

But Meg was only half listening. She was still puzzled over something Gramps had said earlier. Something had to be wrong with the horn clue.

WHAT WAS IT?

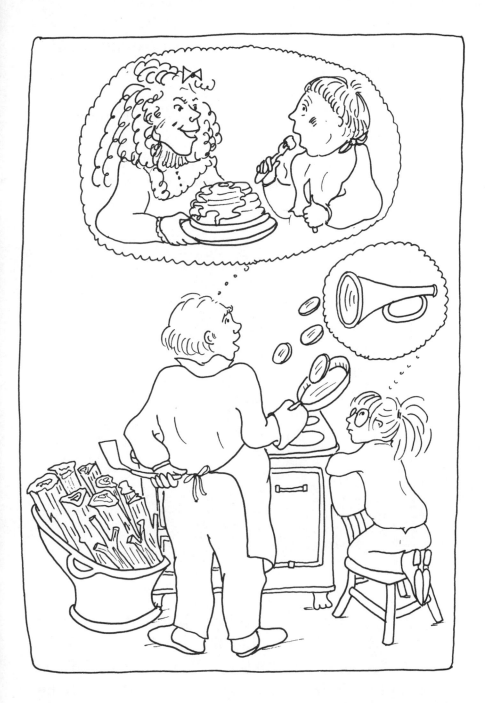

"Wait a minute!" Meg shouted. "Gramps, if you got this bugle for Dad when he was a kid, it *couldn't* be the right horn. It wasn't even *around* when Alice drummed up this whole mystery."

"Guess that's so," Gramps admitted sheepishly.

Meg looked at the clue again. "Whatever you do, don't blow this horn." Remembering another kind of horn, she raced into the living room.

"You wouldn't want to blow this horn, eh, Skip," Meg said as she took the old powder horn off the hook. She pulled off the cap. There was no powder inside, but there was something else. Meg took her tweezers out of her detective kit and slowly pulled out a small, tightly rolled piece of paper.

"I guess I'm not surprised that nobody has looked in there lately," said Gramps. "Maybe you really are onto something, Meg-O. What does it say?"

ucle reeth
tillet ob epep
stol reh ~_?

"I don't know. Does it mean anything to you, Gramps?"

"Never cared much for word puzzles myself," confessed Gramps, "but if you find one of those jig-saw puzzles with the pictures, I'll be glad to help you."

Meg shook her head and sighed. Peter would be arriving soon. She had to solve this mystery fast. Just then the back door slammed and Meg jumped.

"Whew, it's only you," Meg said with a sigh as Liddy came into the room.

"Only me? Only me might help you solve this," Liddy replied as she read the clue. "It looks like a secret-alphabet code. You know, when each letter stands for a different letter in the alphabet."

"Or maybe the letters in each word are just scrambled around," said Meg. She took out her notebook and began trying different combinations.

Before long the door slammed again. Peter was peering over their shoulders.

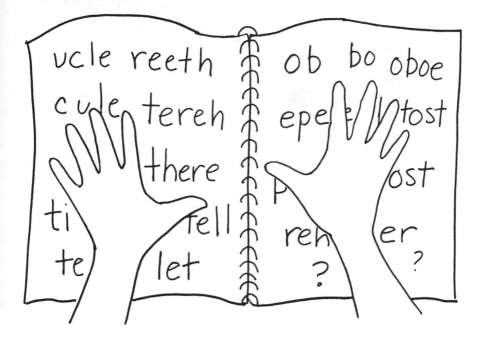

"Here's a clue for you, Nut-Meg, *drop it!*" Peter said. "I can have this solved in no time!"

"I found it, I followed it, and I'll finish it," protested Meg, covering her notes. But not quickly enough.

"What's this? A word puzzle? I could put it on my computer and have it decoded in a flash," Peter persisted. "What's it got to do with a Babe Ruth baseball, anyway?"

Meg snatched the clue back. "Don't bother. I've already figured it out with my own brainpower!"

AND SHE HAD. HAVE YOU?

"Well, what does it say?" asked Liddy, as Peter stomped out of the room. "I counted seven *E*'s, but what does that mean?"

"Nothing. It's not an alphabet code. It *is* a scrambled-letter code. The letters in each word are just mixed around."

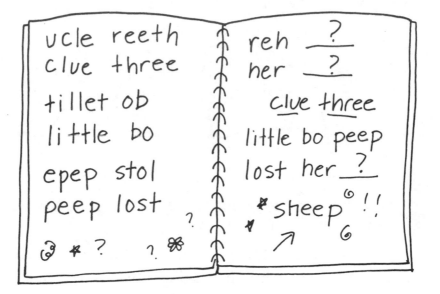

"It says: 'Clue three little bo peep lost her' — her sheep, of course," said Meg.

"Why didn't I see that?" said Liddy, shutting the dictionary.

"Is it something to do with sheep's wool, or an old spinning wheel?" wondered Meg.

"Or a sheepskin?" suggested Liddy.

Meg and Liddy looked high and low. Meanwhile,

Peter was eagerly searching the old photo albums, jotting down notes. He was more nerve-racking than Alice and her crazy clues, thought Meg.

It wasn't until later in the afternoon, when Liddy had gone home, that Meg realized what the answer to the sheep clue was.

DO YOU KNOW WHERE BO PEEP'S
LOST SHEEP CAN BE FOUND?

"Right in front of me all along," Meg sighed. She carefully unhooked the old painting. On the back, tucked tightly between the canvas and the frame, was another small note. But it had crumbled over time.

Meg wrote down what she could decipher.

"Aha! Another scrambled code," said Peter, and Meg jumped. She hadn't heard him come up behind her. "Wait until the guys see that baseball!"

"Stay out of this! You don't even know what it's all about," Meg answered. "Anyway, it's Gramps's baseball."

"I think I've got it unjumbled . . . B-U-D-D-H-A!" Peter raced to the statue in the living room.

But Meg knew he was wasting his time. Taking her notes with her, she slipped off to find the answer to the clue.

WHAT DID THE CLUE MEAN AND WHERE DID MEG LOOK?

27

Peter was way off. It wasn't a scrambled-letter code at all. It was a line from another Mother Goose rhyme. Alice must have meant *tub*.

Meg was scouring the bathroom for clues when Gramps leaned in the door. "Sorry to disappoint you, Meg-O, but you won't find much here. You see, it's like the horn. This bathroom isn't as old as those clues."

"A new bathroom? Then where's the old one?" asked Meg.

"Well, we put a bathroom *in* the house, but we didn't take one *out*, so to speak. Back when I was a youngster, we just had an outhouse. We took baths in an old tub in the kitchen," Gramps said.

"This can't be a dead end," sighed Meg. "There's got to be a solution, after I've gotten this far."

"Alice was cunning," Gramps said.

Meg had to agree.

Later that night, Peter knocked on Meg's door. "Are you still sleeping with Gramps's old stuffed animals? A little babyish, don't you think? I gave up that pathetic old dog years ago."

"What do you really want, Peter?" Meg said suspiciously.

"Hey, Meggy, let's put our heads together on this mystery. I could help you out. For instance, the old outhouse, where Gramps keeps his gardening stuff now. I bet that has something to do with it. Well, see ya in the morning, Nut-Meg."

"I'd already thought of that," Meg said to herself, "but I'd better not wait until tomorrow to check it out. Peter might get there first." When she thought that Gramps and Peter were safely asleep, she pulled her raincoat and boots over her pajamas and tiptoed outside. The air was cool and the ground still damp from rain. Meg flicked on her flashlight and headed for the rickety old toolshed.

The flimsy door swung open. Meg spied a pile of tools and flowerpots and an old rain barrel. Was it an old washtub? It must be — there was a note wedged between the wooden slats! She pulled it out and opened it up.

But instead of reaching for the shovel, Meg sat back on her heels and thought. There was something funny about this clue.

HOW DID MEG KNOW?
HINT: THERE ARE FIVE TELLTALE SIGNS.
CAN YOU SPOT THEM ALL?

1. It was on lined paper. All the other clues were on unlined.
2. It was ripped out of a spiral notebook. None of the others were.
3. The handwriting slanted to the left. Alice's slanted to the right.
4. It said "Clue #4" — but Meg had already found the fourth clue.
5. It had nothing to do with Mother Goose rhymes.

Clearly, this was a fake clue. Someone was trying to throw her off the track. Meg was sure she knew

who . . . and after looking around the toolshed again, she knew where.

Someone had been here recently. There were fresh, muddy footprints and the dust marks showed that the cabinet had been emptied. Ten to one, Peter was inside.

Meg picked up the shovel and scraped it around on the floor, pretending to dig. After a moment, she came up with the perfect plan to turn the tables on Peter.

"Yikes!" she said loudly. "Spiders — a whole nest of them! Come on, Skip, let's split!" She slammed the toolshed door behind her, then tiptoed around the side and peered through the window. In a flash,

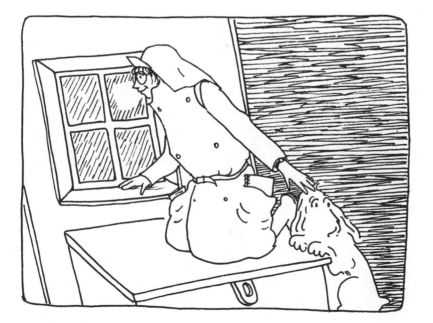

Peter tumbled out of the cabinet and bolted back to the house.

Meg held her breath to keep from laughing. "I'm not scared of spiders," she said to herself, "but you-know-who is . . . Mr. Big-shot Detective! It serves him right for leaving that careless clue."

But, as she headed back to bed, she had to admit she was still no further along in solving the mystery. And time was running out. Mom and Dad would be picking them up the next day at noon.

In the morning, Gramps asked Meg to get some kindling for the wood cookstove. He kept it in a funny-shaped old metal bin. The old bathtub!

Meg searched the old tub for a clue, but there was no note, not a scrap of paper.

"Rats! How else could Alice have left a clue?" wondered Meg as she stirred figure eights in her oatmeal. Gramps always gave her huge spoons. This one had a fancy big *M* engraved on it.

As Meg stared at the spoon, she suddenly had an idea of how a message could have been left.

Just as she suspected, there was something scratched on the bottom of the tub:

"Another clue!" Meg exclaimed. This one looked too authentic to be one of Peter's tricks.

"Gramps, did you have any dogs when you were little?" Meg asked.

"Oh, yes," he replied, "probably a dozen or so. Let's see, there was Nippy and Nicky and Lucky and Flippy and twice as many cats. Gosh, we had a lot of pets — ducks, pigs, ponies, even a parrot."

Then the phone rang. It was Liddy.

"What's happening with the mystery?" she asked.

"Can't talk now," Meg whispered as she noticed Peter at the top of the stairs.

"Is that Lydia-the-Encyclopedia on the phone? Tell her I've got this case just about wrapped up," Peter said as he came down the stairs and glanced over Meg's shoulder. "So what's this latest clue?"

"It has something to do with Little Miss Muffet," Meg teased, "and the spider that sat down beside her, you know, scaring Miss Muffet away!"

"What are you talking about?" said Liddy. "Whatever you do, don't let him get it."

"Don't worry, he's bluffing." Meg hung up. She hoped she was right and that this wasn't all a wild-goose chase. She had some deducing of her own to do — fast. Her only hope was to go back to the beginning.

Deductions
1) All clues have to do with Mother Goose rhymes.

2) All clues are hidden in this house.

3) Clues can only be found in old things because Alice hid them long ago.

Meg studied the old clues, then looked at the new one. " 'The little dog laughed.' If I'm right, it's part of a Mother Goose rhyme, too. And I think I know which one."

WHICH NURSERY RHYME WAS IT?

Meg found the rhyme in Gramps's Mother Goose book.

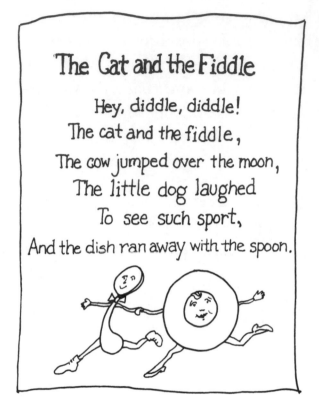

The Cat and the Fiddle

Hey, diddle, diddle!
The cat and the fiddle,
The cow jumped over the moon,
The little dog laughed
To see such sport,
And the dish ran away with the spoon.

"This could lead anywhere! Cat, fiddle, cow, moon, dish, or spoon?" Meg tried not to panic. She took out the old photo of Gramps and Alice that had started her on this investigation and reread Alice's letter and clues.

Peter had been upstairs and down, rummaging through all sorts of old stuff. Was he really onto something and she the one off the track?

Meg was determined to solve the mystery. And as she stared at the photo and clue, it all fell into place.

WHAT WAS THE ANSWER?

Meg ran to her bedroom. Safely tucked under the covers was the old stuffed animal that had once belonged to Gramps. The old toy dog. It was the same one that was in the photograph, the one Peter had teased Meg about.

"The little dog laughed," Meg said to herself. "Of course! 'The answer could be with you right now, but you wouldn't know it anyhow' . . . just as Alice said in the letter."

42

Meg looked at the old toy intently. He was musty and worn. His body was very hard, stuffed with straw.

On his back was a loose thread. It was a different color, as if someone had tried to mend a seam but hadn't done a very good job.

Meg carefully pulled the thread. Sure enough, deep inside the old straw was something you'd never expect to find in an old doggie doll.

The baseball. Just as she had hoped! There was one final note with it, but Meg decided to let Gramps read it.

"What's this?" He woke with a start. "I must be dreaming. My baseball? It couldn't be!"

"It is," said Meg.

"It's what?" Peter burst in.

"It's my Babe Ruth baseball, long lost, and now Meg has found it," Gramps said with a big grin.

"That's right," said Meg. "Alice hid the ball in your old toy dog. With all that hard stuffing, no one ever noticed. She left the Mother Goose clues to help you track it down."

"Amazing," said Gramps.

"Amazing all right," grumbled Peter. "She just got lucky fooling around with those old baby toys."

"Sometimes he reminds me of someone, but I don't know who." Gramps winked at Meg.

"Maybe this will help you remember. It's a note from you-know-who," Meg said, winking back.

August 1928

Dear Georgie Porgie Pudding and Pie,
This time I really made you cry.
Your baseball was never lost it's true,
But I didn't know how to give it back to you.
I thought a mystery would be fun,
With some little clues —
To keep you on the run!
Your cousin
Alice

P.S. I hope it doesn't take
you _too_ long to find it.

"Not *too* long," said Gramps. "Only over fifty years! Wait until I call her and tell her the game is up! And Peter, you be sure to tell everybody back at the Detective Club how Meg-O the supersleuth cracked the case."

Peter groaned. "Oh, all right." Then he even smiled a little.

They heard Mom and Dad's car pull into the driveway. "And solved not a moment too soon," Meg said as she hugged Gramps good-bye.

"You'd better take this along for 'proof,'" Gramps replied, tossing her the baseball.

"Did you catch that, Peter?" Meg laughed. "Wait till the Detective Club sees this!"